W9-AHN-731

PLEASE SAY PLEASE!

Penguin's Guide to Manners

by MARGERY CUYLER

Illustrated by

WILL HILLENBRAND

SCHOLASTIC PRESS * NEW YORK

No part of this publication may be reproduced,
or stored in a retrieval system, or transmitted
in any form or by any means, electronic, mechanical, photocopying, recording, or otherwise, without written
permission of the publisher. For information regarding permission, write to Scholastic Inc., Attention: Permissions
Department, 557 Broadway, New York, NY 10012. Library of Congress Cataloging-in-Publication Data · Cuyler, Margery. · Please say please! :
Penguin's guide to manners / by Margery Cuyler ; illustrated by Will Hillenbrand. – 1st ed. · p. cm. Summary: Penguin teaches his animal friends
how to behave when they are invited for dinner. · ISBN 0-590-29224-2 · [1. Etiquette — Fiction. 2. Behavior — Fiction. 3. Penguins — Fiction.
4. Animals — Fiction.] I. Hillenbrand, Will, ill. II. Title. · PZ7.C997Pl 2004 · [E] – dc21 · 2003005527 · 10 9 8 7 6 5 4 3 2 1   04 05 06 07 08
Printed in Singapore 46 · First edition, April 2004 · The artwork was done in pen, ink, and crayon on vellum. · The text was set in 20-point Hank
and 60-point Mosquito Fiesta. · Design by Kristina Albertson

When friends are invited to Penguin's house for dinner, they should barge right in without knocking.

LET'S EAT!

Is that right?

No, that's wrong.
When friends are invited to Penguin's house for dinner,
they should knock first,
then wait until Penguin opens the door.
HELLO!

When a pig comes to the table,
he should wipe his muddy hooves on the tablecloth.

OH, YUCK!

Is that right?

No, that's wrong.
When a pig comes to the table,
he should wash his hooves first
until they are squeaky clean.
SQUEAK, SQUEAK!

When a hippo sits down for dinner,
she should put her napkin on her head.

HOW PRETTY!

Is that right?

No, that's wrong.
When a hippo sits down for dinner,
she should lay her napkin on her lap.
THAT'S BETTER!

When a lion is served cauliflower,
he should say,
"I hate cauliflower."

EW!

Is that right?

No, that's wrong.
When a lion is served cauliflower,
he should say,
"I'll try some."

When it's time for a bear to eat,
she should grab her spoon
and throw it across the room.

WHEEEEE!

Is that right?

No, that's wrong.
When it's time for a bear to eat,
she should use her spoon to taste her honey.

STICKY-POO!

When an elephant drinks milk at mealtime,
he should spray it all over the table.

SPLAT!

Is that right?

No, that's wrong.

When an elephant drinks milk at mealtime,

he should sip it quietly, a few gallons at a time.

SSSSSSiP!

When a chimpanzee wants more to eat,
she should grab what she wants.

GIMME, GIMME!

Is that right?

No, that's wrong.
When a chimpanzee wants more to eat,
she should say,
"Please pass the bananas."
HEE-HEE!

When a rhino makes a joke at the table,
he should talk with his mouth full.

BLAH! BLAH!

Is that right?

No, that's wrong.
When a rhino makes a joke at the table,
he should swallow what's in his mouth first.

GULP!

When a parrot has to go to the bathroom,
she should fly from the table without being excused.

GET OUT OF THE WAY!

Is that right?

No, that's wrong.
When a parrot has to go to the bathroom,
she should say, "May Polly be excused?"

SQUAWK! SQUAWK!

When a giraffe eats leaves for supper,
she should burp to show that she's happy.

BUR–R–R–R–R–R–R–P!

Is that right?

No, that's wrong.
When a giraffe eats leaves for supper,
she should try to control herself.

OH, MY!

When it's time for the guests to go home,
they should knock over the chairs and run for the door.

ME FIRST!

Is that right?

No, that's wrong.
When it's time for the guests to go home,
they should say,

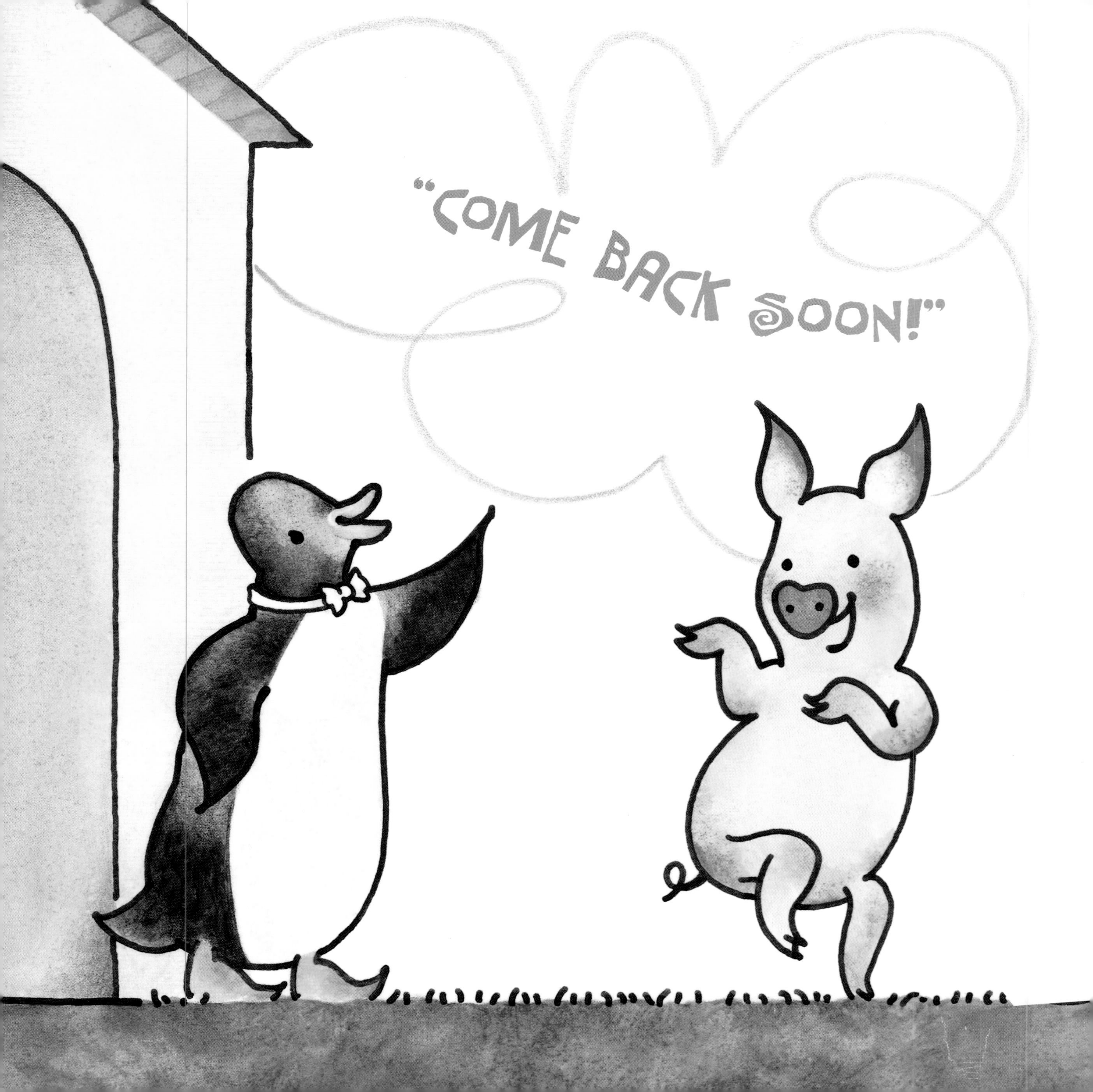
"COME BACK SOON!"